PUFF

DUE D1100218

Dick King-Smith served in the Grenadier Guards during the Second World War, and afterwards spent twenty years as a farmer in Gloucestershire, the county of his birth. Many of his stories are inspired by his farming experiences. Later he taught at a village primary school. His first book, *The Fox Busters*, was published in 1978. Since then he has written a great number of children's books, including *The Sheep-Pig* (winner of the *Guardian* Award and filmed as *Babe*), *Harry's Mad, Noah's Brother, The Hodgeheg, Martin's Mice, Ace, The Cuckoo Child* and *Harriet's Hare* (winner of the Children's Book Award in 1995). At the British Book Awards in 1991 he was voted Children's Author of the Year. He has three children, a large number of grandchildren and a number of great-grandchildren, and lives in a seventeenth-century cottage, only a crow's-flight from the house where he was born.

Some other books by Dick King-Smith

Dick King-Smith
Dumpling

Illustrated by Jo Davies

PUFFIN BOOKS

PUFFIN BOOKS

Published by the Penguin Group
Penguin Books Ltd, 80 Strand, London WC2R 0RL, England
Penguin Putnam Inc., 375 Hudson Street, New York, New York 10014, USA
Penguin Books Australia Ltd, 250 Camberwell Road, Camberwell,Victoria 3124, Australia
Penguin Books Canada Ltd, 10 Alcorn Avenue, Toronto, Ontario, Canada M4V 3B2
Penguin Books India (P) Ltd, 11 Community Centre, Panchsheel Park, New Delhi – 110 017,
India
Penguin Books (NZ) Ltd, Cnr Rosedale and Airborne Roads, Albany, Auckland, New Zealand
Penguin Books (South Africa) (Pty) Ltd, 24 Sturdee Avenue, Rosebank 2196, South Africa

Penguin Books Ltd, Registered Offices: 80 Strand, London WC2R 0RL, England

www.penguin.com

First published by Hamish Hamilton 1986
Published in Puffin Books 1995
Published in this edition 2001
5 7 9 10 8 6

Set in 15 on 22pt Times New Roman Schoolbook

Printed in China by Midas Printing Ltd

British Library Cataloguing in Publication Data
A CIP catalogue record for this book is available from the British Library

ISBN 0–141–31297–1

"**O**h, how I long to be long!" said Dumpling.

"Who do you want to belong to?" asked one of her brothers.

"No, I don't mean *to belong*," said Dumpling. "I mean to BE LONG!"

When the three dachshund puppies
had been born, they had looked
much like pups of any other breed.

Then, as they became older, the two brothers began to grow long, as dachshunds do. Their noses moved further and further away from their tail-tips.

But the third puppy stayed short and stumpy.

"How *long* you are getting," said the lady who owned them all to the two brothers.

She called one of them Joker because he was always playing silly games, and the other one Thinker, because he liked to sit and think deeply.

Then she looked at their sister and shook her head.

"You are nice and healthy," she said. "Your eyes are bright and your coat is shining and you're good and plump. But dachshunds are supposed to have long bodies, you know. And you haven't. You're just a little dumpling."

Dumpling asked her mother about the problem.

"Will I ever grow really long like Joker and Thinker?" she asked.

Her mother looked at her plump daughter and sighed.

"Time will tell," she said.

Dumpling asked her brother, Joker.

"Joker," she said. "How can I grow longer?"

"That's easy, Dumpy," said Joker. "I'll hold your nose and Thinker will hold your tail and we'll stretch you."

7

"Don't be silly, Joker," said
Thinker.

Thinker was a serious puppy. He
did not like to play jokes. "It would
hurt Dumpy if we did that."

"Well then, what shall I do,
Thinker?" asked Dumpling.

Thinker thought deeply. Then he
said, "Try going for long walks. And
it helps if you take very long steps."

So Dumpling set off the next morning. All the dachshunds were out in the garden. The puppies' mother was snoozing in the sunshine.

Joker was playing a silly game pretending that a stick was a snake.

Thinker was sitting and thinking deeply.

Dumpling slipped away through a
hole in the hedge.

Next to the garden was a wood, and she set off between the trees on her very short legs. She stepped out boldly, trying hard to imagine herself growing a tiny bit longer with each step.

Suddenly she bumped into a large black cat which was sitting under a yew tree.

"Oh, I beg your pardon!" said Dumpling.

"Granted," said the cat. "Where are you going?"

"Oh, nowhere special. I'm just taking a long walk. You see, I'm trying to grow longer," and she went on to explain about dachshunds and how they should look.

"Everyone calls me Dumpling," she said sadly. "I wish I could be long."

"Granted," said the black cat again.

"What do you mean?" she said. "Can you make me long?"

"Easy as winking," said the cat, winking.

"I'm a witch's cat. I'll cast a spell on you. How long do you want to be?"

"Oh very, very long!" cried Dumpling excitedly. "The longest dachshund ever!"

The black cat stared at her with his green eyes, and then he shut them and began to chant:

"Abra-cat-abra,
Hark to my song,
It will make you
Very long."

The sound of the cat's voice died away and the wood was suddenly very still.

Then the cat gave himself a shake and opened his eyes.

"Remember," he said, "you asked for it."

"Oh, thank you, thank you!" said Dumpling. "I feel longer already. Will I see you again?"

"I shouldn't wonder," said the cat.

16

Dumpling set off back towards the garden. The feeling of growing longer was lovely. She wagged her tail madly, and each wag seemed a little further away than the last.

She thought how surprised Joker and Thinker would be. She would be much longer than them.

"Dumpling, indeed!" she said. "I will have to have a new name now, a very long name to match my new body."

But then she began to find
walking difficult. Her front feet
knew where they were going, but her
back feet acted very oddly. They
seemed to be a long way behind her.

They kept tripping over things,
and dropping into rabbit holes.

They kept getting stuck among
the bushes. She couldn't see her tail,
so she went round a big tree to look
for it and met it on the other side.

By now, she was wriggling on her tummy like a snake.

"Help!" yapped Dumpling at the top of her voice. "Cat, come back, please!"

"Granted," said the witch's cat, appearing suddenly beside her. "What's the trouble now?"

"Oh please," cried Dumpling, "undo your spell!"

"Some people are never satisfied," said the cat. Once more he stared at her with his green eyes.

Then he shut them and began to chant:

"Abra-cat-abra,
Hear my song,
It will make you
Short not long."

Dumpling never forgot how wonderful it felt as her back feet came towards her front ones, and her tummy rose from the ground.

She hurried homewards, and squeezed her nice, comfortable, short, stumpy body through the hole in the hedge.

Joker and Thinker came galloping across the grass towards her.

How clumsy they look, she thought, with those silly long bodies.

"Where have you been, Dumpy?" shouted Joker.

"Did the exercise make you longer?" asked Thinker.

"No," said Dumpling. "But as a matter of fact, I'm quite happy as I am now.

"And that's about the long and the short of it!"